I dedicate this book to Claire, my wife and muse. I've been making wacky food images to entertain her since we got married in 1961. A big thank-you to our daughters, Lisa and Nina, and to our grandchildren, Ethan, Simon, and Daniela, for joining in the fun with healthy food. Special thanks to Morty Matz, Sam Roberts, Lena Tabori, and Jim Muschette, and to Peter Rubie, Deirdre Jones, and Véronique Lefèvre Sweet for your help bringing *Foodie Faces* to life. —BW

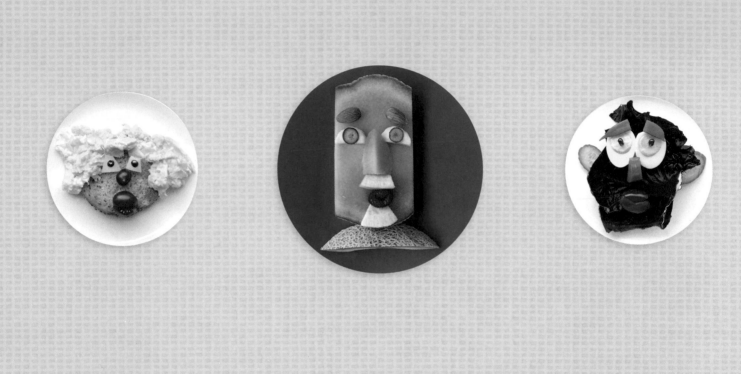

ABOUT THIS BOOK

The illustrations for this book were created using photographs of fresh fruits, vegetables, grains, and more. This book was edited by Deirdre Jones and designed by Véronique Lefèvre Sweet. The production was supervised by Erika Schwartz, and the production editor was Annie McDonnell. The text was set in Just Tewll Me What Regular, and the display type is P22 Stanyan Bold.

• Little, Brown and Company • Hachette Book Group • 1290 Avenue of the Americas, New York, NY 10104 • Visit us at LBYR.com • First Edition: June 2020 • Little, Brown and Company is a division of Hachette Book Group, Inc. • The Little, Brown name and logo are trademarks of Hachette Book Group, Inc. • The publisher is not responsible for websites (or their content) that are not owned by the publisher. • Library of Congress Cataloging-in-Publication Data • Names: Wurtzel, Claire, author. | Wurtzel, Bill, author. • Title: Foodie faces / Claire Wurtzel and Bill Wurtzel. • Description: First edition. | New York : Little, Brown and Company, Hachette Book Group, 2020. | Audience: Ages 4–8 | Summary: "Faces made out of everyday fruits, vegetables, grains, and more teach young readers about emotions and healthy eating"— Provided by publisher. • Identifiers: LCCN 2019022090 | ISBN 9780316423540 (hardcover) | ISBN 9780316423519 (ebook other) | ISBN 9780316423533 (ebook) • Subjects: LCSH: Emotions—Juvenile literature. | Nutrition—Juvenile literature. | Health behavior—Juvenile literature. • Classification: LCC BF561 .W87 2020 | DDC 152.4—dc23 • LC record available at https://lccn.loc.gov/2019022090 • ISBNs: 978-0-316-42354-0 (hardcover), 978-0-316-42353-3 (ebook), 978-0-316-42350-2 (ebook), 978-0-316-42355-7 (ebook) • Printed in China • APS • 10 9 8 7 6 5 4 3 2 1

Foodie Faces

Bill and Claire Wurtzel

LB

Little, Brown and Company

NEW YORK BOSTON

There are lots of ways to feel.

Sometimes I feel SAD.

Other times I feel **HAPPY**.

My face turns red when I'm ANGRY.

Sometimes I growl when I'm GRUMPY.

I don't want to look at anyone when I feel SHY.

But sometimes I feel FRIENDLY and ready for fun.

I feel **WORRIED** when something is wrong.

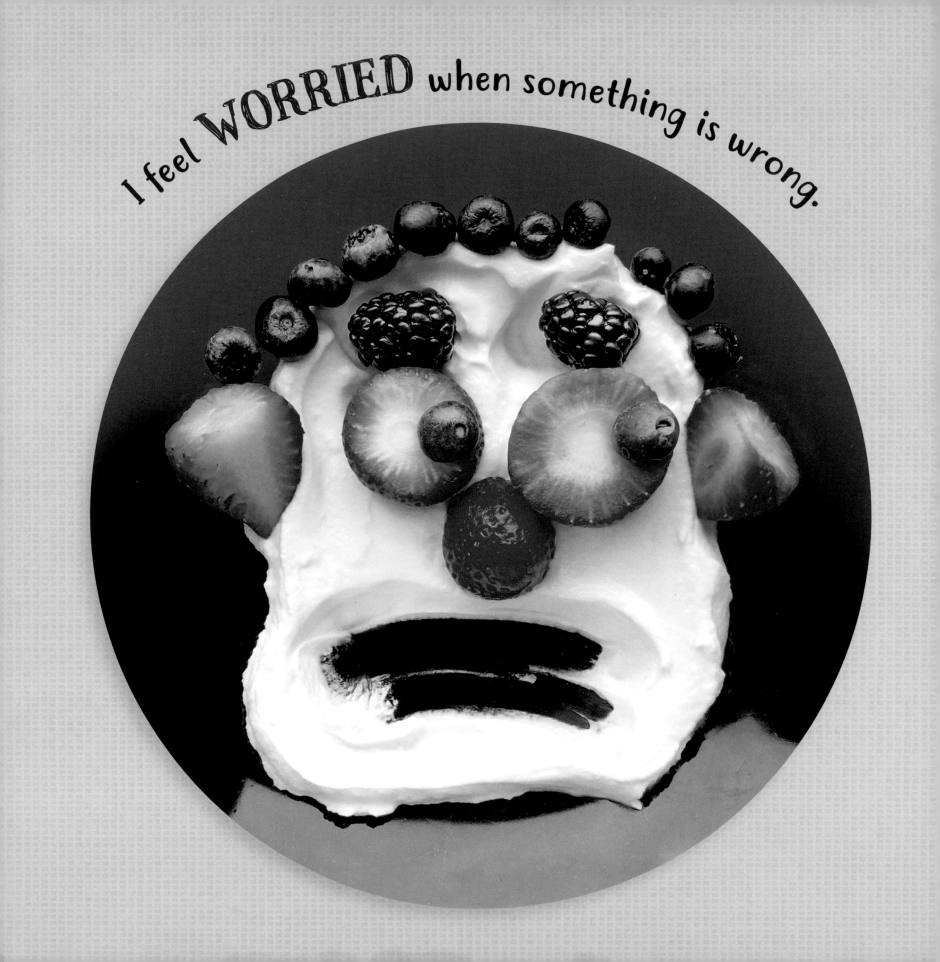

I like it better when I feel cool and CONFIDENT.

I like to be SURPRISED.

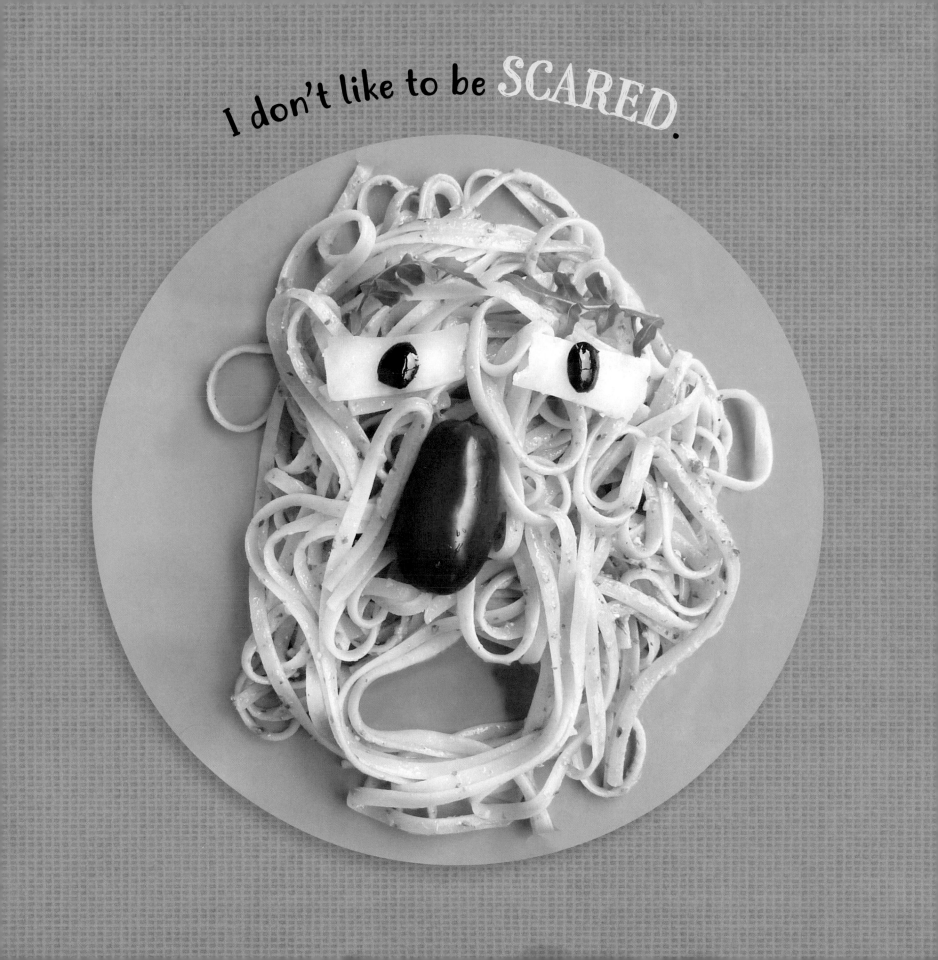

I don't like to be SCARED.

I make funny faces when I feel SILLY.

I feel EMBARRASSED when I make a mistake.

When I see something interesting, I feel CURIOUS.

Or maybe I just feel CONFUSED.

One minute I might be MOODY.

And the next minute I'm as CHEERFUL as can be!

Sometimes I feel **EXCITED**.

Sometimes I feel CALM.

I feel **BORED** when there's nothing to do.

I feel **PLAYFUL** when there are fun things to do.

All these feelings are making me HUNGRY.

Now I'm ready for bed, because I'm SLEEPY.

A Note from Claire

Photo by Nina Wurtzel

When I was a child, my mother made funny objects out of leftover dough. After Bill and I got married, he was inspired to continue making these whimsical creations for me, using fruits, vegetables, grains, and more. About ten years ago, I encouraged Bill to start photographing his creative plates before I gobbled them up, and several books (including the one you're reading now) came out of that idea.

Children connect with their feelings when they look at faces showing a range of human emotions. And building a vocabulary for feelings helps us understand and cope with them. As you read this book together, if you're a mom, dad, grandparent, or caregiver, share a time when you felt happy, and a time when you felt sad. If you're a kid, look at the faces in this book and say which one represents how you're feeling. Are you happy? Grumpy? Silly? Are you bored? Excited? Hungry?

Both adults and children tell Bill and me that the faces in our books look like neighbors, aunts and uncles, friends, and more, and they are amazed that just a few pieces of food can evoke strong emotions such as joy, sadness, and curiosity. Bill and I hope you enjoy reading and sharing this book and that it helps start discussions about feelings and healthy eating in your family.

Build Your Own Foodie Face

You'll need a round piece of pita bread, a stick of string cheese, lettuce, two baby carrots, two blueberries, two slices of cucumber, a grape tomato, and two wedges of a clementine. Follow the below steps to make a silly face. If you don't have the right ingredients at home, that's okay. Try making a face out of the foods you *do* have. Then eat it all up when you're done!

1. **2.** **3.** **4.**

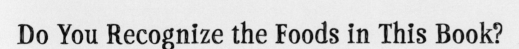

Do You Recognize the Foods in This Book?

Go back and see if you can spot these tasty fruits, vegetables, grains, and more:

- **Bagels** and **breads** can create the base of a face. (So can **waffles** and **pancakes**.)
- **Bananas** make great mouths.
- **Carrots** are perfect for eyebrows.
- **Lettuce** and other **greens** make the best hair.
- **Blueberries**, **blackberries**, and **raspberries** can turn into eyes. (So can **radishes** and **cucumbers**.)
- **Strawberries**, **tomatoes**, and **peppers** can become ears, mouths, and noses.
- **Cantaloupe**, **mangoes**, and **watermelon** make round faces.
- **Almonds**, **sunflower seeds**, and **cashews** make perfect teeth.
- Spread **yogurt**, soft **cheese**, or **hummus** wherever you need to create a funny shape.

That's not all. There are even more foods in this book! Which ones can you find? Which ones would you like to try?